Curious George®

A Home for Honeybees

Adaptation by Julie Tibbott
Based on the TV series teleplay
written by Ron Holsey

Houghton Mifflin Harcourt
Boston   New York

For information about permission to reproduce selections from this book, write to Permissions, Houghton Mifflin Harcourt Publishing Company, 215 Park Avenue South, New York, New York 10003.

ISBN: 978-0-544-23777-3 hardcover
ISBN: 978-0-544-23791-9 paperback

Design by Afsoon Razavi

www.hmhbooks.com

Printed in China
SCP 10 9 8 7 6 5 4 3 2 1
4500450623

AGES	GRADES	GUIDED READING LEVEL	READING RECOVERY LEVEL	LEXILE ® LEVEL
5–7	1–2	J	17	470L

George and Steve liked to build things.
"You two are good builders. Like bees!"
said Betsy.

George was curious.
Bees could build things?

"Bees make honeycomb inside their
hives to store honey," Betsy said.
She gave some to George and Steve
to taste.

Betsy showed them her poster from Earth Day.
Bees build hives in trees to lay their eggs and store honey.

All the bees follow a queen bee.
She's the biggest bee in the hive.
Worker bees go from flower to flower
getting nectar and pollen to make honey.

The honeycomb was very sweet.
When Betsy left for dance class,
George and Steve ate the whole thing!

They needed to find more honeycomb!
George and Steve went to the park to
look for a beehive in a tree.
"Be careful! Bees can sting!" Steve said.

George could not find a hive.
But he found something else.
He saw a beekeeper at the Earth Day
festival in the park!

"This is a beehive," the beekeeper said.
"I built it myself. It works the same
way as a hive in a tree."

The bees make
honeycomb on the
frames in the top box.
The box on the bottom is where the
queen bee lives and lays her eggs.

"You can build your own beehive,"
the beekeeper said. "Then you can get
more honeycomb!"

They went back to George's house to get started. Steve drew plans for the hive. George thought building boxes would take a long time.

George tried to use drawers.
Some drawers didn't fit together!

But a kitchen cabinet would make a
great beehive!
Surely the man with the yellow hat
would not mind.

George knew
where to get frames.
He and Steve put all the parts
together.
Their beehive was ready to go
back to Betsy's house.

Now they needed to find some bees.
George had an idea.
Maybe if their hive had flowers, the bees
would move in.

But just then, Betsy came home.
"I'm sorry we ate all your honeycomb,"
said Steve. "We built you a hive to make
more."

Steve and George were worried
Betsy would be angry.
But instead, she looked happy.
"This is the best present ever!"
Betsy said. "Besides, that piece of
honeycomb was for you. I've got
lots more."

What a relief!
Betsy's project was not ruined AND
there was more honeycomb.
Everyone was happy.

Well, almost everyone.

Sweet Sculptures

Bees build their hives out of beeswax, which they produce with their bodies to make honeycomb. You can build things with all kinds of materials—even dough! Get a grownup to help you make this edible play dough.

What you will need:
1/2 cup honey
1/2 cup peanut butter
Powdered milk (do not add water)

What to do:
Mix together the honey and the peanut butter. Add enough milk powder to make the dough the right consistency. Have fun creating bees, flowers, or whatever you want—and when you are done playing, you can eat your creations!

Be Like a Bee

Did you know that bees can dance? Their dance tells other bees where flowers are located. When they are done collecting nectar and pollen from the flowers, they use their antennae to smell their way back to their hive. Each bee colony has a unique odor so bees can tell it is their home. Now you can have antennae just like a bee.

What you will need:
A plain headband
Chenille craft stems (pipe cleaners)
Small Styrofoam balls

What to do:
Twist two pipecleaners together to make each antenna. Using yellow and black ones will make you look like a real bee!

Twist the two antennae around the top of the headband, several inches apart. Make sure they stand up straight.

Pop a Styrofoam ball on top of each antenna. You may color the balls black first, if you like.

Now go outside and smell the flowers—and do a little dance!